"To make old Bones
You have to go easy
Don't spread yourself too thin
To go far

Don't bust your Rump
Know when to give
Some tender Kisses
under a corner of blue sky."

—Serge Gainsbourg

To Pierre and Achille, my two lazy bums,
and to our suspended hours.

— Christine

Originally published in French in 2016 under the title *Mon chat Boudin* by Éditions de la Martinière,
a division of La Martinière Groupe, Paris. This edition published in 2017 by Abrams Books for Young Readers,
an imprint of ABRAMS. All rights reserved. No portion of this book may be reproduced, stored in a retrieval system,
or transmitted in any form or by any means, mechanical, electronic, photocopying, recording, or otherwise,
without written permission from the publisher.

Printed and bound in France
10 9 8 7 6 5 4 3 2 1

Abrams Books for Young Readers are available at special discounts when purchased in quantity for premiums
and promotions as well as fundraising or educational use. Special editions can also be created to specification.
For details, contact specialsales@abramsbooks.com or the address below.

ABRAMS The Art of Books
115 West 18th Street, New York, NY 10011
abramsbooks.com

My Lazy Cat

CHRISTINE ROUSSEY

Abrams Books for Young Readers
NEW YORK

This is Boomer.
Mom found him on our front porch one day,
fast asleep and spread out like a pancake.
When she brought him inside, he curled up, smiled,
and fell asleep right on my feet!
That's when I knew he was my cat.

Boomer is tubby and chubby. He's all puffed up like a balloon!
He has two pointy ears that stick out from his round head and
four paws that are too small for his body.

Boomer is my best friend.

He gives the best hugs and purrs like a tiger.

But Boomer is LAZY.
One word can't explain how lazy he is!

He's a slug,
a sloth,
a slacker.

A lounger,
a loafer,
a lazybones.

He snoozes and slumbers, dozes and drowses.
No one does it better.

Then there's me. I don't have a minute to waste!
I have judo, swimming, yoga, painting, and pottery.
Knitting, soccer, and biking with my friends.

I have a full day and I can't be late!
I don't have time to cuddle, Boomer.
Get out of my way!

I have to get ready for my day.

First I put on my bathing suit and pack my bag for swim class,
but Boomer uses my swim cap for a sleeping cap!

Then I gather my paintbrushes and pencils,
but Boomer is lying on my art project!

Boomer, move! It's almost time for soccer.
Last I grab my cleats—but then . . .

BAM! I trip over Boomer.
All my stuff goes flying across the room while Boomer snores.

What a mess. Now I'll miss soccer for sure.
I feel like crying.

But then I look at Boomer, and Boomer looks at me.
And we laugh and laugh!

Boomer wants to show me something.
He leads me to the backyard.
We plop down in the grass and look at ladybugs.
We listen to the wind blow through the branches
of the big pine tree.

I'd forgotten that pine tree was even here!

We wander over to the pond and listen to the *drip*, *drip* of the water, the *bloop*, *bloop* of the fish,

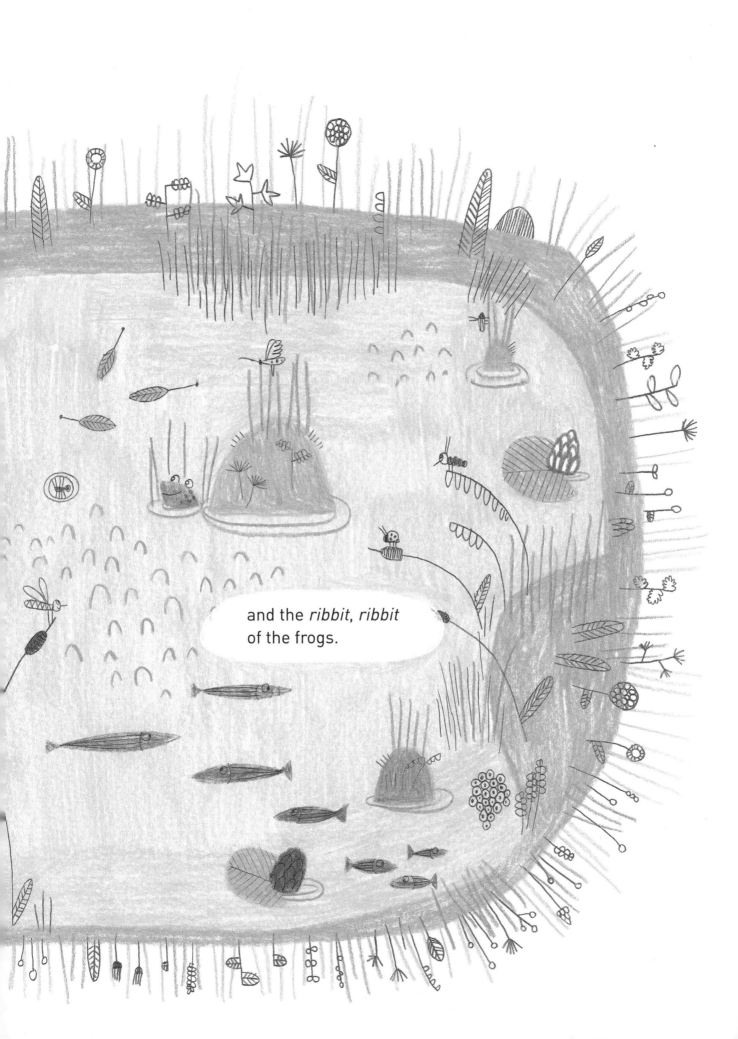

and the *ribbit, ribbit* of the frogs.

Our stomachs gurgle.
So we munch on berries and cherry tomatoes
and pick plums and pears off the trees.

I haven't done this since I was on vacation
at Grandma and Grandpa's house.
Now we are full and sleepy.

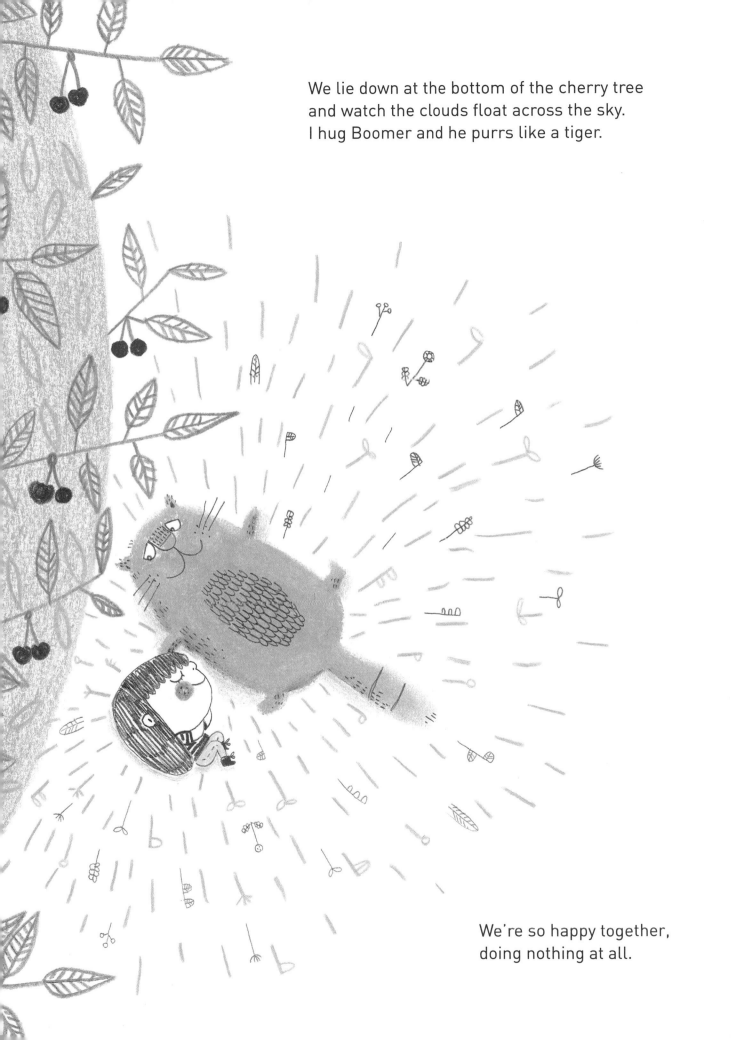

We lie down at the bottom of the cherry tree
and watch the clouds float across the sky.
I hug Boomer and he purrs like a tiger.

We're so happy together,
doing nothing at all.

At dinner, Mom and Dad ask me,
"What did you do today?"
"Nothing," I say. And I smile.

Cataloging-in-Publication Data has been applied for and may be obtained
from the Library of Congress.
ISBN 978-1-4197-2602-6